THE VEILED UNIVERSE

THE VEILED UNIVERSE

Cosmic Tales of Science Fiction

Rob Garnet

The Veiled Universe: Cosmic Tales of Science Fiction

This edition first published in 2019

ISBN (Paperback): 978-93-5396-100-8

Edited by Vrinda Baliga (vbaliga@gmail.com)
Cover design by Aditi Shah (aditishah0@gmail.com)
Typeset, printed and bound by Red Knight Books

ABOUT THE AUTHOR

Rob is an engineer who has spent years working in various global companies. He is a keen traveller who has so far covered sixteen countries. This helps fulfil his desire to understand the local language and customs, and realise the further we go, the closer we humans come to each other.

He has penned professional articles and is a frequent public speaker on management and human resources. He has also written short stories in science fiction and fantasy, some of which can be read on his website. He believes that the future of humanity is bright; there are many more scientific discoveries yet to be made.

With over two decades of experience working in the fields of science, he understands the anxiety this poses to the general reader who is at risk of getting lost in the jargon. Therefore, his foremost desire is to simplify the concepts of science and present them in the form of narratives that the readers will not find overwhelming. He spends hours thoroughly researching his selected themes and then weaves his tales around them. He hopes that these stories will ignite the imagination of the readers and take them into uncharted realms of science fiction.

You can learn more about him and his books at https://robgarnetauthor.wixsite.com/robg

Follow him on Instagram @robgarnet

INTRODUCTION

Our quest for knowledge will never be complete. Scientists work on theories that explain observations. Experiments performed either strengthen or disprove the theories. However, as the name suggests, these are just theories and a new observation may disprove what we have held to be true for hundreds of years. This book is not a scientific or religious treatise. Instead, it picks up some of the common and popular scientific themes and weaves stories around it. You do not need to be a student of science, but you do need to set your imagination free to enjoy them.

These stories will challenge all that you know of the universe and force you to ask the question 'What if…?'

Rob

CONTENTS

QUANTUM REALITY

"This is Trailblazer checking in. Commander Daniel reporting. We are now 1.57 light years from origin. The reactor is recharging. All systems are green. Attaching formal report of day 2257." Daniel listlessly tapped out the commands on the touch panel to send the message on its way. His work for the day was done.

Life aboard the ship had not been taxing at all, except for the take-off and a brief period navigating through the Oort cloud at the outer edge of the solar system. He had completed more than six years flying the ship, all alone in the darkness with stars and random comets for company. The novelty of the journey had worn out quite quickly, especially since most ship functions were handled by the on-board computer and the artificial intelligence. His main role was limited to ensuring the AI itself was functioning as programmed. Feeding the guard dog, as he liked to put it, though the AI itself had all the personality of a house cat.

For all the hype that had been built around it back on Earth, the whole voyage to find exotic particles and search for extra-terrestrial life had been a big waste. None of the experiments had yielded any results so far. The mysteries of physics remained mysteries.

***

Thresto entered the chaos in the control room.

"Talk to me, Xuco," he ordered the program director. "What was so important that you called me from the board room?"

"Uh, sir… the ship has reached the final boundary. There was a power failure and we are still struggling to restore the program."

"Impact?"

"The program cannot advance further than this point. We can run limited local scenarios but we cannot add the next full-set till power is restored."

"Does the human know he cannot proceed further?"

"Can't tell for sure, sir, but it's unlikely. However, when his ship hits the boundary and stops moving in… fifteen minutes, then he will know."

"Are we still broadcasting?" asked Thresto, his eyes running over the control station.

"Yes, we are. Three point five trillion people are tuned in."

Thresto ran over the alternatives quickly. This was the most popular show ever, having run for over five thousand years. Maybe it was time to kick things up a notch. He had limited choice but there were a couple of people he could trust to play the role he had in mind.

"Is Melou over in the newsroom? Get her over here. Right now. She has to take a trip. Let's make programming history, guys!"

***

"Hello, Daniel."

Daniel nearly fell off his seat, spilling his morning cuppa.

"What the…?" He looked about the cabin wildly.

The figure, clad in a gold and silver suit, looked so incongruous that he stared at it goggle-eyed for a full minute. A face, dark and classically beautiful, looked back at him from across the control panel. There was a twinkle in her grey eyes.

"Who? Wha..? How…?" He could not get a full word out however much he tried.

"All in good time, Daniel."

Where did she come from? How does she know my name? He fell silent, trying to regain some part of his composure.

"I am Melou, and I am here to ask you to return home. There is nothing more for you to discover in deep space."

Daniel pushed himself up. "Now, look here. Who do you think you are to come on my ship and give me orders?" *Really?* He mentally chided himself. A beautiful woman appears mysteriously aboard my ship in the middle of deep space and all I can say is this?

"I can't really explain." She seemed to be mocking him. "You wouldn't understand even if I were to tell you everything in minute detail. Your primitive mind will simply disregard it."

"Yeah?" He dabbed at the tea on his suit. "Try me."

"All right then, as you primitive humans say. But I warn you again, there is no way you'll comprehend any of it."

"Primitive, huh?" Her supercilious attitude was beginning to grate on his nerves. "May I remind you that we humans have reached this far in space."

"Space," she smiled in a condescending way he found infuriating. *Who did she think she was?* Melou walked slowly around the cramped cabin, absent-mindedly touching various objects. "Space does not exist." She grimaced and shrugged in a very human manner. "Where you are today is the limit beyond which humans cannot be allowed to go. It is the 'boundary'."

Daniel gaped at her. He still could not make up his mind if he was dreaming all this.

She stepped up to him and looked him in the eye. "Everything you see around you is simulated. For millions of years we have nurtured Earth and its inhabitants. You see, I am from a race called Crisceods. We... created... your reality, this reality, piece by piece."

"Uh-huh?" He could hear her words, but his mind seemed to have turned to mush for all the sense they were making.

"I told you, you wouldn't believe me."

He shook his head as if to clear his mind. "You mean besides the fact that you belong to a race of super beings who created us? You really haven't given me any empirical facts or evidence." His confidence rose as he spoke. For all he knew, she was some sort of a simulation herself.

"Okay. Tell me, has your mission in space been successful? You came here to examine what you call 'neutrinos' in deep space, away from the interference of Earth's atmosphere, and to look for the next level of particles after the discovery of …what do you call them…'binary-mesons'? Such quaint names. Have you found the particles you came looking for?"

"No, I haven't," he admitted, reluctantly.

"That is because they do not exist, Daniel. None of your famed theoreticians and physicists cared to question why they kept finding new particles every time they split the atom?" She shook her head and laughed. "That Olxu. He was the one who came up with this idea of a never-ending series of particles for your people to split and give funny sounding names to. Yeah, we did have lots of fun with that one. Seriously, who came up with the idea of the up-quark and down-quark?" She paused and became serious. "Anyway, there are no particles. In a way, however, your m-theory was correct. It is all energy. Your reality was created out of pure energy. If humankind had not given up on that theory, you might have discovered us by yourselves. We managed to divert you away from that path."

"There are no particles for me to find here? But where do the neutrinos come from?"

"Oh, Daniel. Space, the solar system, the galaxies—none of them exist except in the simulation. Why do you think they have all been placed so far apart that humans can never hope to reach them? The speed of light is a real limitation we imposed to keep you from venturing too far."

"I don't believe you. You are making this up. Show me some evidence."

"Evidence, huh? Like in your physics experiments? Sure. Look outside the porthole. See with your own eyes what the Crisceods can create."

Daniel turned around and looked out. His eyes widened in total disbelief. He could see San Francisco outside, the Golden Gate Bridge resplendent on a bright summer morning. All of a sudden, the scene changed to a war and he was right in the middle of it. Looking at the uniforms on the fighting men, he vaguely registered that this was the American civil war of the nineteenth century before a bullet grazed his shoulder. He felt the wound, and his hand came away wet with blood. Then the scene changed again, and he stood on the cold surface of a dead planet. Confusion clouded his face as numerous incongruous scenes played out one after another, until finally he closed his eyes, completely disoriented. When he opened them again, he found himself collapsed on the floor of his ship, his chest heaving with emotion, blood dripping from the wound on his arm.

"You see we can transform your reality anyway we want. I have brought you to your ship now, back right where you started." She waited for a reaction but once more, he found himself speechless with shock. She shook her head again in exasperation. "Anyway, look, I am here to terminate your journey. We have indulged you far enough. I'm afraid you can't be allowed to go further."

"Terminate my journey? How? Why?"

"Earth's development has been one of the longest running dramas on my planet. It was enjoyable especially when especially when binge-watched, but now we need more theatre, or the audience will get bored. It is nothing personal. You turn around, go back to Earth and that's it."

"Yeah? And what if I tell them all that I have learned from you?" He knew she would see through his bluff.

"Oh, come on, Daniel. Do you really think they will believe you? They will think this voyage into deep space muddled your brain and put you under… what do you call it… psychiatric evaluation. Now that will be a good episode."

That was true. No one would believe him. He would be confined to an asylum, in all likelihood for the rest of his life.

"Okay look. I will offer you a choice—turn back now and face whatever happens on Earth, or we destroy your ship here and now and no one will ever know what happened to you. Either way, the show will go on."

***

"Audience poll! Now, Xuco! How many viewers think he will take the second choice? Offer them a live visit to Earth as the prize."

***

"Wait! Wait! Give me some time to think!" Daniel was panicking. Insanity or death—these were hardly choices at all! "One last question. How do I know I am not a simulation?"

"You really don't but honestly we needed real emotions not programmed. We did not create you," answered Melou.

The ship lurched as it banged against an invisible barrier. Daniel fell to the floor, but Melou stood there looking at him with pity.

"I am sorry, Daniel. We are out of time. Make a choice."

Daniel looked up at her. There really was no choice. Six years of work had gone down the drain… but what difference did it make? What difference did any of it make? He believed Melou. There was no reality. His life was a lie. Every human who was alive or had ever lived and even those not yet born—all their lives were a lie. Science was a lie. Even God was a lie. Maybe one-day humans would figure out the truth anyway. He imagined eight billion human beings discovering that that there was nothing more to life than being part of a galactic soap opera.

If I go back, everyone will think I am a liar, or worse, a coward. There was no choice.

***

"Don't you ever spring this on me again!" Melou screamed at Thresto. "I am a journalist. Your best journalist, not some dumb starlet in your goddamn show."

"Relax, Melou. We have everything in control. Trailblazer is history. In a few years, when the humans back on Earth hear nothing more from Commander Daniels, it will be yet another big mystery for which they will have no answers. In the meantime, this gives us time to clean out the glitches. More importantly, we have a winner from Vaotis who is eager for their trip to Earth. You will be the first to interview him. I don't have to tell you, your work on the ship was brilliant. And remember, human lives are inconsequential. It is the show which is important."

***

Kul sat back in his chair, laughing heartily. He could not believe how well the entire episode had played out. These Crisceods were as gullible as the Earthlings were. Creating the power failure had been a stroke of genius. The ratings for the show would have jumped. Maybe next time Kul could create a big bang event. Let's see how the Crisceods respond to that, he thought chuckling.

It all made for good theatre.

THE CRAB NEBULA

"**O**kay, folks, look through your telescopes or binoculars," I said, gloomily. I desperately wanted to avoid this particular lesson, but I did not have a choice. Once every year I was forced to face my darkest memories. "Your instruments have been focused just above Orion near Beta and Zeta Centauri," I continued, keeping my voice level. "That is where you will find the oblong object called the Crab Nebula."

The students dutifully looked through their telescopes. Jamie, as usual, had forgotten his, and I cast a reprimanding eye at him as I walked around helping the others until I was satisfied they had succeeded in their quest.

"Good. Now who will tell me about its history? Anyone?"

I was pleased to see Anita lift her eyes from the telescope and raise her hand.

"Crab Nebula got its name because the first drawing of it resembled a crab," she said. "It is located 6500 light years away and was first observed more than a thousand years ago as part of a supernova explosion."

Supernova. Yes. Death and destruction.

"That is correct," I said. "It is believed to be the remnant of a massive explosion which took place approximately 7500 Earth years ago. The central star exploded and destroyed the entire system. It also formed a neutron star in its place which gives off massive amounts of radio energy." I glanced at Anita who had raised her hand again. "Yes?"

"You said it destroyed the entire system, but I read that no one really knows if there actually was an explosion or what happened during the purported explosion or even if there were any planets in the system. Isn't it true that we can only guess the size of the star and may never know what actually happened?"

She was smart, that girl. I forced a smile. "You're right, of course, Anita. However, we have enough information to draw conjectures, and who knows, we might be correct." I turned back to the class. "That's it for today. Assemble your photographs and submit your paper on the structure and status of the Crab Nebula by the end of this week. Dismissed."

***

I sat at my desk trying to focus on grading the papers. A knock on the door interrupted me. I looked up to see Anita at the door.

"Yes, Anita? What can I do for you?"

"I'm sorry sir, but I had a question?"

I waved her to a chair. "Go on then."

"Back in the class, you sounded pretty convinced about the star system being destroyed in the supernova. And…"

I stiffened. "And?"

"And you seemed somehow emotionally affected by it. Sir, do you know something the books and astronomers and Wikipedia does not?"

I stared at her. Her question was direct and she met my eyes unflinchingly. I averted my gaze and shuffled the papers on my desk. She did not budge.

"Well, you might be right," I said finally, with a sigh. "You want to hear a story? It might take a while."

She nodded eagerly.

"Many thousands of years ago, there was a star system," I started. "It was called Xeccor. It was a large system with twin suns and fifteen planets. One of the planets, called Aelud, was populated and two more had been colonised. Aelud had a very advanced civilisation and its people managed to travel to other planetary systems, including ours."

"You're kidding!" Her eyes were wide with excitement.

"Do you want to hear the story or not, young lady?"

She nodded.

"The remarkable thing about the people of Aelud was their longevity," I continued. "They lived for thousands of Earth years and well, one of the outcomes of their technological progress and long life was that they started running out of fuel and energy. Their needs far outstripped the supply even from their two suns and what they could scavenge from other star systems. They were running out of options. Their best scientists were enlisted to find an answer to their predicament. Large-scale evacuation to another world was ruled out. They did not have the fuel to carry every living soul to the nearest habitable planet. Enclosing their star inside a shell to harness every last bit of radiant energy was a possibility, but that required more material than the fifteen planets and their moons could provide. In fact, it required a billion times more material. Finally, one scientist came up with a radical proposal—"

"What was his name?"

"Whose name?"

"The scientist's, of course."

"Why do you want to know his name?" I raised my eyebrow. "Okay, his name was Ejaw, happy?"

"Ejaw." She tried the name, apparently satisfied. "Go on then."

I gave her an exasperated look. "So, Ejaw came up with an idea to dramatically increase the output of their sun. His idea was to assimilate the smaller sun into the larger one thus increasing the total mass available for fusion reaction. He calculated that the rate of reaction would also increase exponentially, potentially providing Aelud with enough energy to last a million years."

"Whoa! A stellar collision!"

"Not exactly. What he wanted to do was to increase the gravitational attraction between the two suns in the binary system and cause them to join. His proposal, while radical, was also quite simple. He intended to push the first planet in the Aelud star system inwards towards the larger star. As the planet was consumed by the sun, the sun's gravity would increase marginally—just enough to pull the smaller star closer."

I stopped to take a sip of water. The physics behind the proposal had been so simple and yet so elegant. Nevertheless, I realised Anita would need more details.

"As you have learned in our astronomy classes, the suns and the planets in a star system are held together in a delicate balance. It takes millions, if not billions, of years for their individual masses, along with other planetary objects such as moons and asteroids, to settle into stable orbits. Their gravity, as I explained, keeps them at just the right distance from each other. Ejaw's plan, therefore, was to disturb the stable orbits just enough to cause a stellar merger. You're with me so far?"

She nodded wordlessly. I knew she was picturing it—the graceful dance of celestial bodies in a faraway star system.

"So then," I continued, "they brought their largest ships, along with all their reserves of fuel, for one monumental attempt. One chance was all they were going to get, and they had to make it count. And you know what? They managed to nudge the planet just enough out of its orbit, that the sun captured it and pulled it in. It did not happen in a day, to be sure, but eventually their main sun had just the right amount of gravity and the first object it pulled was its twin. The rest of the planets were far enough not to feel the increased attraction and were safe for the moment. The scientist planned to use the same technique of pushing using large ships to bring the rest of the planets back to stable orbits once the main part of the experiment was completed and they had enough energy to spare."

Anita listened open-mouthed. "Did they achieve their stellar merger?"

"They were well on their way to achieve their goal, but Ejaw and the other scientists had overlooked one small complication in their experiment. Stellar rotation. The smaller star was not just pulled in; it spiralled inwards and slammed into the main star resulting in a massive explosion, a supernova. The entire system and every living soul within many light years was consumed in a giant fireball. All that remains of that phenomenal experiment is the Crab Nebula." I turned away and blinked back my tears. I could feel her watching me.

"How do you know all this, sir?"

"I'm not sure I can tell you everything, but one person escaped the explosion—Ejaw. He had taken a ship far out of the system to observe the effects of the gravitational shift from a distance and measure the changes. The first wave of the explosion threw him and his ship even further away. He drifted alone, angry and heartbroken, for many years before he found a planet and settled down there with his grief. He blamed himself for the loss of fifty billion lives and decided to spend his remaining life honouring their memory and teaching others about the wonders of the universe."

We sat silently across from each other.

Then Anita stood up and came around the desk to me. She touched my shoulder and said softly, "You were wrong. You were not alone. Two more people escaped the disaster. My parents were on an off-world mission at that time. They managed to find their way to Earth and spent their lifetime searching for the cause of the destruction of their beloved world. I carried on with their quest when they passed away. And today at last I have learned the truth." She sighed deeply. "I forgive you, Ejaw, and I think it is time that you forgave yourself."

THE HARVEST

He hoped the harvest would be better this year than the last. He could really use the money. The crop looked quite healthy and he was sure it would fetch him a good price. Moreover, there was the larger picture to think of. The food shortage had exacerbated over the last few decades and farms like his were one way of keeping the human population from starving to death. He wandered through the carefully tended fields. Row upon row of bods, almost ripe for harvest. Pipes snaked around them: blue pipes for water, green pipes for nutrients, and black pipes, buried under the soil, to carry away the waste. Nutrients were then recovered from the waste stream thus keeping his operational costs low. The entire field was inside a large converted structure with multiple layers of air filtration to ensure the foul air outside did not stunt the growth of his crop. He liked spending his time here—in the clean air, with artificial yellow lights and a peaceful atmosphere.

He checked the various instruments and made minute adjustments. The central computer was supposed to control most of the processes, but it had been acting up lately and he needed to monitor the crop personally. Manual supervision of such a huge area was difficult and he invariably had to skip checking on significant portions of the fields.

The fields were set in four sections depending on the variant planted. The blue field was the most valuable to him. The most expensive variety, which could potentially fetch him three times the standard rate at the auction. At the very bottom of the scale was the red field, the paler variety. Its yield was generally lower, but it was easier to sell.

He entered a section that he had not checked in several months. He clucked his tongue to see some of the lights had broken leaving portions of the field in darkness. The field looked less tended as well. Then, he noticed a gap in the neat lines. *Was that an empty space? What the...?* He strode over. Yes. Someone seemed to have broken and removed at least one, maybe even two, bods from the blue batch. The gap was stark, with the blue and green pipes hanging free, discharging water and nutrients on the ground in a muddy puddle.

He stood there staring at the incongruous scene. A small commotion in a corner nearby startled him. "Connie?" he bellowed. That girl would be the death of him. "Connie!"

A pair of blue eyes in a round face framed by golden hair peeked out from behind two hanging bods.

"Yes, Papa," she said tremulously, knowing she was in for a scolding.

"Did you remove the bod? How many times have I told you this is not a place for you to play?"

"But he was fully grown and…and he opened his eyes!"

"They do that sometimes, but that does not mean you can go and remove them, okay?" he said sternly. "And for the nth time, they're not 'he' or 'she', they're just bods." The dehumanised nomenclature was there for a reason. How could one farm them otherwise? "Now, where have you taken it?"

She pointed to the storage area piled with sacks. He took her hand and walked her over.

"Why do we grow them like this, Papa?"

"I've explained this to you several times, Connie. We are facing the worst famine of the last one hundred years. No crops can grow in the contaminated air and soil outside. Even the animals died out. So the government permitted us to grow these bods in a controlled environment for consumption. They are a very good source of nutrition."

"But what about these... these... people? Don't they deserve to live?"

"That's just it, Connie. They are not 'people', and they are not alive in the real sense. They are not conceived but bred in a lab, like the one across town. They have been genetically modified to metabolize synthetic supplements and they cannot reproduce. Besides, like I said, they provide us with heaps of nutrients and solve the world's food problem. So, it's all good, okay? Now tell me, what have you done this time?"

"Nothing," she replied in a small voice, her head down.

"Connie?"

"I just wanted to take him…it out for a walk. And I think you are wrong. They are alive. They can love. He…it recognises me by now. It responded to me, and it also has a mate."

He shook his head absently, squinting at the storage area, looking for signs of the bod. "They don't take walks, honey, and they cannot love. I doubt they have enough intelligence to think. At best, you can think of them as primitive savages. How many times have I told you to stop making up stories about them?"

Connie knew better but she kept quiet. They reached the stack of sacks and he went around it, following the characteristic smell of the bod. He could not see the bod on the ground and stepped in deeper. Suddenly, something fell on him from the top. Something slimy, slippery and very strong. He had barely recovered before something bit a large chunk off his arm. He screamed, finally catching sight of the bods that had attacked him. There were two, not one. The sharp claws and teeth shocked him as they sank into his soft flesh. He heard slithering noises from another corner. There were more. He screamed again. "Connie! Get out of here! Call for help! Go!" Connie ran.

He could sense more of the bods coming after him. Oh God! If these get out it will be a massacre. He kicked out with both legs, pushed himself up and ran, blood flowing from the wounds on his arms and legs. He needed to get to the diesel. The cans were lined up in a corner to fill the generator. He hoped some of them were full. Thankfully, they were.

He looked back desperately. The two bods hesitated, watching him from the safety of the sacks, but he was sure they would come after him. He twisted off the cap of one can, then the next, and the next. Gathering the cans in his hands, he limped over to the water supply and dumped the contents in. The liquid was quickly carried over to the bods in the fields, which started twisting as the strange liquid invaded their systems.

He felt around in his pockets for his lighter and flicked it on, just as the two bods charged forward, and crashed into him. As they dug their teeth and claws into him, he tossed the lighter into the tank. A bright orange and blue flame leapt up and travelled through the pipes to the bods. They writhed and thrashed as they burned on their crosses. The two bods who had attacked him dashed back into the storage stack. He stared after them in surprise. He had thought they would bolt in the other direction, away from the flames. Did they think the sacks were safe from the fire? Just goes to show they have no intelligence. His attention was drawn back to the field as hundreds of bods screamed in agony, their flesh melting away in the fire. Never knew they had voices. The entire field blew up in a massive fireball. This was one time he was happy he would not be harvesting his crop.

***

As the fire blazed, lighting up the evening sky, two bods crawled out of the side door, stumbling away into the darkness. They carried a small, wailing bundle in their arms.

THE LAST
HEIST

Skani leaned across the table conspiratorially, his voice a whisper, "I tell you, we pull this off and we will never have to work again. Ever."

I took a swig from my glass and popped a couple of nuts in my mouth, chewing thoughtfully. Skani always had some "brilliant" scheme or the other up his sleeve. Most were hare-brained and invariably had at least one insurmountable obstacle, if not more. On the other hand, it was not as if I had any other job in the pipeline. I had barely escaped the patrol ships of the Baxu in my last run carrying contraband Olent fur. Now, the Baxu had increased the bounty on my head to twenty thousand shards. A bounty this big had me worried. But it was also more than a little gratifying, an acknowledgement of my skills.

"Go on then," I said.

Skani glanced around nervously. The bar was dark, and our seats were at the very back, right next to the kitchen door. I was the only female here, but people knew to leave me alone. Even the waiters and the bartender never approached unless called. Satisfied that no one could overhear him, Skani leaned even closer until his long purple nose was nearly touching the grimy table. "There is a white dwarf star called Lucy twenty-five light years from here. Word on the street is that it crystallized as it cooled down." He looked at me meaningfully as if the significance of this was obvious. .

"I know something about Lucy, of course," I said, noncommittally. "It has crystallized into a massive diamond. So?"

"So?" he repeated, his voice rising with incredulity. "So?" He forgot he was supposed to be whispering. Realising his mistake, he bent down once more. "It's not just any diamond, Meki. It's trillions of trillions of carats of a single diamond. The largest diamond ever discovered this side of the galaxy. Word is that it is almost flawless. Just imagine if we can get a few hundred carats, we can retire tomorrow."

It was enticing but there had to be a catch somewhere in this fantastic scheme. "If the diamonds are inside the sun, how are they mined?" The question had never occurred to me before. Probably because I had not been planning on mining stars for diamonds.

"That's the beauty of it, Meki! Other suns expel gases during solar flares, Lucy spews diamonds. In essence, the entire system is full of diamonds. The Konai who claim that system, and the Baxu, who protect it, collect the diamonds from a safe distance. The queen of Varga Prime had her entire crown made from a single piece. Six thousand carats! And there is plenty more out there, but they keep a close tab on the quantity mined to keep the prices high. So, all we need to do is to find our way to the system and collect a few for ourselves. The system is primarily guarded by automated systems. It will be easy."

If it was so easy, why had no one else tried it earlier? "What's the catch?"

He had the grace to look sheepish. "The Baxu, of course. They keep a fleet of ships on standby to deal with any intruders who do make it. They destroy any ship found near the system and execute every person on board on the spot. They have a sophisticated sensor grid ringing the entire system. But their reputation has been far more effective in scaring people off."

"And you think we can just waltz in unannounced and gather the booty?" I wondered what he had been smoking.

"Listen, three months ago, two ships managed to sneak in through the barrier. They even managed to gather the stones, but the Baxu ships caught the thieves within ten light years and obliterated them. They have the fastest ships in the known universe."

I shook my head in disbelief. "Let me get this straight. You know the Baxu have the fastest ships in the galaxy and they obliterated these other ships, and yet you want me to try the same stunt? Are you out of your mind or do you have a death wish?"

He pretended to be offended, widening his three eyes and putting his pudgy hand over his heart. "Death wish? Who? Me? I like living well enough, thank you very much, Meki. Listen, I can get you in. I have some connections. All you need to do is get us away from the Baxu before they can locate us. We will have a window of almost fifteen minutes before they can reach us."

I paused, considering. If he was confident he could get us in… maybe the whole thing was not as impossible as it sounded.

"So? What do you say, Meki? Can you do this? Can you? We'll split fifty-fifty." He was almost bouncing in his seat, like an eager puppy.

I finished my drink and looked around. This bar was the dingiest one this part of the city, even if it was the safest. I was tired of constantly looking over my shoulders, forever running from the Baxu. Maybe this was a chance to thumb my nose at them and escape this drudgery. I could get to Rohini V. That was well out of the reach of the Baxu Empire. I leaned back in my seat and put an arm over the backrest. "Maybe."

That was enough for Skani. We got down to the planning. We would need a decently fast ship, capable of travelling at least at the speed of light and with manoeuvrability; enough to zigzag through the Konai's mining operations. I would need one more item. A black hole with relativistic jets. Skani need not know the entire plan just yet.

***

Two months of solid preparations later, we were holding point just inside Lucy's star system, hiding behind a cluster of six moons of the outermost planet waiting for a gap in the sensor grid.

Skani jumped from screen to screen waiting for the moment to arrive. His hands twitched intermittently as he swung between glee and anxiety. He needed to calm down if he was to be of any use in this caper.

"You are getting on my nerves," I snapped. "If I tell you how we will escape, will you sit down and be quiet?"

"Yes. Yes. Yes." He looked around, found the co-pilot's seat and sat down. His fingers tapped an incessant pattern on his knees.

"We will collect whatever diamonds we can find during the next flare. You need to fill our holds as fast as possible. No more than thirty seconds, understood? Based on my understanding of the Baxu's response, that will leave us with fifteen minutes to make our escape."

"Fifteen minutes. Yes. Yes. Yes."

Maybe this whole scheme had been a big mistake. Skani was coming unhinged.

"I found us an escape route. There is a black hole, eighteen light years from here. Our ship can cover that distance in twelve minutes. That black hole has a rotating accretion disc which spews out jets of plasma at relativistic speeds. Now, I have mapped out the timing of the jets and there is one scheduled in exactly fourteen point five minutes. So, you collect the diamonds, we hightail it to the black hole and ride the jet. This jet ride will last just a few hours. We will be gone by the time the Baxu reach the black hole. Even if do reach in time, they will never be foolhardy enough to try to follow us. Everyone knows these relativistic jets of plasma are a one-way ticket. They can spit you out so far, you will never have the fuel to return. Even if they do follow us on another jet, they will find the landing spot empty. We will be long gone."

The plan was elegant. I had installed sixteen shields on the ship, enough to withstand the superhot plasma and the travel at hyper-speed. We would be halfway across the galaxy, and the Baxu ships would be eating our space dust. I had even charted the course based on the direction of the last few jets, and by my calculations, the jet would take us all the way to the Morle system, two thousand light years away. From there it was a hop, skip and jump to Rohini V. I was exceptionally pleased with my plan.

"Ride the jet? Ride the jet! That's your grand plan? That's like riding lava being spewed by a volcano and hoping it will not fry you! Oh great! And you were accusing me of having a death wish!"

"It will work. Trust me."

"Yeah. Yeah. Like I have a choice. We are already in the cauldron, what's a little more heat." He continued to mutter to himself, but like I had hoped, my plan had shocked him into docility.

***

We raced out of the Konai system at the speed of light, our cargo hold full of diamonds. At least half a ton of them. SOB, we were rich! Stupendously rich!

The automated defence systems had kicked in almost as soon as we entered, but we managed to dodge the worst of them. The wide-span radar showed six Baxu ships coming after us, but we have a decent head start.

We reached the black hole exactly as planned. It was a medium-sized black hole, and our scientists had determined that with the jets being given off at regular intervals, the black hole was unlikely to grow any further. The accretion disc at the event horizon, a swirling mass of gas and plasma, was a delight to look at.

We saw an upheaval in the disc and got ready. The jet was forming. I kept my hands on the throttle. I needed to match the velocity of the jet precisely so our ship could stay just in front of it without being destroyed. We had to ride it much like a surfer rides the waves at the beach. Nice and easy.

I accelerated just as the jet exited the accretion disc, took up position just in front of it and…whhhooooosh! The ride was brilliant. Space twisted around us as we broke the light barrier and then some. The ship was buffeted horribly and we held on for our dear lives. With no way of fixing our position, I prayed my calculations had been correct. There was nothing more to do but wait.

Two hours later, I put the ship into a steep dive and accelerated away from the jet.

"Where the hell are we?" asked Skani.

I looked through the portholes and then at my instruments and then through the porthole again.

"I… I… don't understand. I worked everything out. We should have been at Morle. But…"

The space outside was empty. It was bereft of stars, planets and any type of celestial body. I got up and squinted through the porthole. There were some points of light in the far distance. Going back to the console, I adjusted the long-range telescopes. The points resolved into galaxies. Unfamiliar ones.

"The jet must have changed direction. Inside its sphere of influence, time and distance have no meaning. We have been thrown clear of the Milky Way. Thousands, maybe even millions of light years away. There is no way we have enough fuel to go back. We… we are lost in space."

"We are lost in space. Lost in space. Lost in space." Skani stared at me blankly.

I looked out into the dark void. We had no supplies whatsoever. I had insisted we travel light. After all, I had figured, we would have more than enough shards to buy all the food and supplies we wanted in Morle. Now, all we had was a cargo hold full of diamonds. Except, we could not eat diamonds. Nor could we run our ship on them.

Skani's hands were twitching again. This time I did not reprimand him. My hands were shaking, too. He had been right about one thing: we would not be working again. Ever. This was our last heist.

THE NINTH PLANET

The ship lurched as it struggled against another onslaught of gravitational waves. Andrew held on to the console with both hands, waiting for the ship to stabilize. There had been no warning as usual, and he had not managed to fasten his restraining belts in time. On his left, his second officer, Cristina, was more composed, securely held in her seat.

"15% stronger than the previous one," Andrew muttered. "I still cannot locate the source, dammit!"

"Boss, these readings just don't make any sense." Cristina showed him her portable screen. "Look at the intensity of the gravitational attraction in this area. It has been strengthening over the last few days, yet there is nothing out here."

Andrew scratched his head, poring over the data presented. It was this same gravitational mystery that had initiated their mission in the first place. The orbits of the planets in the solar system had consistently indicated an influence other that of the sun, the planets, their moons and other celestial objects. Pluto was too small to cause this effect and had already been classified as a dwarf planet. No other candidate had been found till date to account for the observational anomaly or to hold the distinction of being the ninth planet of the solar system. Every mathematical model had agreed that there had to be more mass than observed for the solar system to be stable, yet, there it was—a stable system with eight planets and a yellow sun.

Their ship was the first one to venture beyond Neptune in search of the mysterious mass which surely must exist to account for the anomaly. So far, they had found nothing but for a few large boulders adrift in space and everlasting emptiness. Now, there were these cursed waves all from a seemingly invisible source. He walked over and peered intently through the large, reinforced portholes. Nothing. The space outside was empty and featureless.

"I just don't understand it," he replied. "All of these lines are intersecting at this one point 55 million miles away and yet there is nothing out there. At least nothing that our instruments can detect…" his voice trailed off as he branched off in another thought.

The door opened and Sara entered the operations centre.

"Lee's been injured. He hit his head when the last wave hit us. Kevin's with him." She met Andrew's eyes. "You gonna continue this foolhardy mission even after six of your crew are lying in sick bay? This is foolhardy."

"Careful, Sara," said Cristina in a warning tone. "That's the mission commander you're talking to."

"Not for long, if this continues. You will destroy the ship. We should turn around now. This search is pointless."

"Oh yeah?" Andrew retorted. "Then I am sure you have found the source of these gravitational waves. Do let us into the secret, will you?"

They should never have brought Sara along, he reflected, ruefully. A computer system specialist, she was clearly out of place in a deep space mission. But his boss, the mission director, had been adamant about including her. She would help them chart out the best paths and mapping solutions, he had insisted.

Andrew had been forced to acquiesce despite his deep misgivings. And he had been right. Sara had been petulant and disruptive throughout the ten-month journey, getting on everyone's nerves. Maybe throwing her out the airlock, as some of the crew had suggested, was not such a bad idea after all.

"I don't understand why both of you are obsessed with this useless mission. We have already established that this region of space is empty. There is no ninth planet hidden beyond Neptune. This whole journey was just a colossal waste of time," said Sara, making a face.

Andrew bit back a cutting response. Fortunately, Cristina came to his rescue.

"Calm down, Sara. The absence of planetary bodies does not mean this region is empty. We still cannot explain the level of gravity, can we? Get down to mapping the graviton flows we have seen yesterday. The fate of the crew and the ship may well depend on it." Cristina was calm but firm, and her voice brooked no argument. As Sara moved off to her station reluctantly, Cristina turned back to her readings. It had to be out here, the planet they had come to discover. But they were fast running out of time.

Suddenly, alarms blared across the cockpit and amber lights lit up every console. Even as Andrew gave rapid instructions to the piloting crew to control the violently bucking ship, he noted from the console that the mysterious forces had increased tenfold in intensity.

"Warning! Warning!" the disembodied voice of the computer called over the cacophony of the alarms. "The ship is exceeding the stress safety threshold. Reduce velocity now."

"What the hell do you think we are trying to do?" Andrew finally exploded. "Cristina! The force is too strong. We are being pulled in. Cut the engines. Deploy Mayday beacons and send a distress signal back to Europa station!"

"Roger," she acknowledged. As the engines turned off, the ship visibly quietened down. "Sara, get me the latest flows, now!" The squiggly lines on her display reminded her of a spider's web. They were caught like flies.

"Boss, The ship is being pulled towards the convergence point of the waves."

"I can see that, but it does not help us, does it? Get me some data I can use. And reverse the engines. We are still moving forward!"

"Engines reversed. Forward motion down to five hundred mph."

"Warning! Warning!" the computer called out. "Fuel burn rate is 125% of recommended maximum. Reduce speed now."

Then, a moment later: "Warning! Warning! The ship is exceeding maximum stress levels. Reduce speed now."

"It's no use, boss! We can't fight it. Stopping all engines!" Her display showed that hull stress was continuing to build.

"Warning! Warning! Imminent hull collapse! Prepare for evacuation!"

Cristina wiped the sweat from her brow and looked outside the porthole. "There! Did you guys see that! Oh, wow!"

"What? What do you see?" Andrew ran to the porthole. The space outside was empty as ever.

"There is something out there. Something gigantic. Like a…a planet. Only, it was like… a shadow. Ethereal. I saw it only for an instant."

***

It grew silent again. It had been a mistake to allow its attention to drift. Unfortunately, it could not always control its actions. Like now, when gravity was increasing, and the ship was in danger. It had made the mistake and the human ship was caught in its gravity and were in grave danger. It had to make things right and protect the humans. They were fragile, much like the planet on which they had been raised.

***

"I can't see a thing." What was this dark planet nonsense? Their sensors still could not detect any solid objects.

"Boss! It was out there. Believe me!"

"Cristina, focus! We need to find a way out of this! Sara, prepare the crew to head to the escape module!"

"It's changing!" exclaimed Sara. "The flow lines are changing. I need your help, Cristina!"

"Oh man! These lines are emanating from the point where I saw the object. Look at this new flow.

It's completely changed configuration, as if... as if..." Cristina's voice failed her.

"As if what, Cristina!" shouted Andrew as the computer called out another warning. They were out of time.

Cristina turned towards him, a wild look in her eyes. "As if it changed orientation in an instant. It is not possible. That... that object was monstrous. Nothing can move that fast!"

She was being delusional, concluded Andrew- invisible objects in space indeed. But she was still their best bet. "Does this new orientation of gravity help us?"

"What? Oh... yes! Yes! Give me manual control of the ship. I think we can bounce off using the waves and escape." Andrew authorised the controls to be released to her.

"Increasing forward thrust, both engines at fifty percent. I'm gonna bounce the ship off like a pebble off the surface of a lake. Hold on, everybody." Her eyes reflected her manic belief.

"What? Are you crazy?"

"No. I am not. I know this will work."

"You know this will work? How? You will get us all killed!"

"It… whatever is out there. It told me!" screamed Cristina, her lips pulled back in a grimace as the ship picked up speed and bucked forward like a racehorse released from its paddock.

***

The ship skimmed over an unseen surface, and then its direction changed again as it was cast away with enormous force back towards Uranus.

Cristina watched the speed indicator climb into the red zone. This was so much faster than their engines were capable of pushing the ship. I hope we stay in one piece, she prayed, as G-forces kept her pinned to her seat scarcely able to breathe.

They zipped towards Uranus, got caught in its gravity and were catapulted again, this time towards Jupiter, two billion million away.

She could barely see the display through her half-closed eyes, but her mind registered that the ship's computer had extrapolated their course. They were going back to Earth. Finally, she passed out just like the rest of the crew

✳✳✳

It watched them leave as it resumed its standard position and found a new course for itself to follow. It did not know its own age. Time did not pass the same way for it as for humans. But asked to hazard a guess, it would have said a few billion years. It did not know how it came to be, but it had seen the formation of the solar system. It could see, smell, and observe every change in the solar system. It could capture light and radiation and interpret them. Now, when the humans had come so close, it found that it could sense their emotions and in turn affect those too.

Over millions of years, it had observed evolution on three planets. On one of them, the third planet, life had progressed faster than on the other two. It was, however, compelled to stay hidden in the farthest reaches of the system. If it tried to come any closer to the planet called Earth, it would have destroyed the delicate forces which held the solar system in gravitational equilibrium. It liked the name the humans had coined for the invisible, mysterious mass which made up much of the Universe and its own self—dark matter. But the humans did not know that it was organic. It was alive.

ORIGINS

There are a hundred thousand million stars in the galaxy with new ones being born and older ones dying every day. The galaxy also has countless number of planets. Over the course of billions of years since the Big Bang, across thousands of light years of space, life should have evolved across thousands of planets.

J'ron had studied evolution for over three hundred years, working her way through the limitations imposed on her research because her species was isolationist, abhorring contact with other races from other planets. They had not always been so, but having interacted with beings from other planets over thousands of years, they had learnt that though such contact brought them a wealth of knowledge, over time it also brought assorted complications. Handling politics across hundreds of planets meant squandering precious resources in the pursuit of transient peace. After a time, it became easier to deny further associations and be content in their own world. This approach had worked well for her planet for over four centuries.

J'ron was living in an age of contentment. Resources were plentiful and the people were happy, pursuing arts and leisure. Scientific curiosity was not discouraged, but people of T'ref'ker believed they had discovered everything there was to know about the Universe. There were no more secrets left in physics or chemistry. They could harness limitless clean energy, turn rock into gold at will and had proven that it was impossible to travel through time.

However, J'ron struggled to come to terms with the final unanswered question of existence. How did life come to be? Science explained the building blocks of living organisms, but it never explained their origins. After centuries of futile search, and with the growth of isolationism, this problem had been largely forgotten. With no means to go back in time, investigating the origins of life had been deemed too difficult after a point and all efforts on this front had been abandoned on T'ref'ker.

However, J'ron had persevered with her research. She had devoted her adult life to studying all databases and ancient texts regarding contacts with alien races. She drew up a chart of the galaxy mapping every single point where intelligent or basic life had evolved.

The result was a painstakingly drawn-up map with details of evolution, further classified by time, location and type of civilization among other parameters. Detailed examination had revealed a pattern. There seemed to be a common element, a common point. At first, she had not believed her own findings. Modern people on T'ref'ker had evolved over time from less-intelligent species; this was something even the youngest child on T'ref'ker knew as a given and never questioned. However, her research seemed to point in a different direction, to suggest an alternate origin of life. She had thrown away her notes, refusing to give credence to results that conflicted with such deeply held beliefs. It simply could not be! She had to have made some mistake in her research. Yet, the results had continued to haunt her till, finally, she had returned to her studies once again. It was many years later that she had finally concluded that she had been right. There was a pattern to the origins of life!

She spent the next few years, carefully collating her findings into a dossier. It contained inescapable conclusions based on incontrovertible data. The logic was irrefutable. The findings were genuine.

She took her dossier to eminent scientists; people she considered close colleagues if not quite friends. They laughed at her, most refusing to even look at her notes, leave alone discuss her logic. She persisted, reaching out to old professors, friends from her university, even chance acquaintances from her first job. She was rebuffed every time.

Finally, she resolved to reach out to the science council directly as her last resort. If they refused to listen to her then she would be out of options.

Her credentials helped her one last time to get a hearing with a select committee of the council. She prepared herself well, going through her folder multiple times until she was absolutely sure of her approach. She hoped she would be able to convince at least one or two scientists on the council who would approve further research and maybe even allow her the use of a ship to go out into the galaxy to prove her theory.

They laughed at me! They actually laughed at me! Coming out of the council chamber where she had been given an audience for barely five minutes, she raged inwardly. The philistines! Nincompoops! Idiots! If they will not listen to me then I will do this myself! All I need is a ship. It need not be very big or very fast, just enough to get me off this damned planet!

With all interstellar flights banned and indeed no usable ships capable of interstellar flight available on the entire planet, she knew she would have to find another way. There was one option—the Emergency Cosmic Space Station on the Southern Pole, which provided services for spaceships from other planets needing assistance—the only allowance made in the planet's strict laws. She hoped to be able to persuade a friendly captain to take her on board.

That had been two months ago. She had travelled hundreds of light years on board a freighter from the planet Delmir, following the leads indicated by her star charts. She had exhausted all her money and found nothing. Three of the points had been empty space. It did not make any sense to her. Was the nodal point not fixed but travelling across space?

She had finally figured it out. The point was not in a specific star system but on a rogue planet, which had broken away from its orbit around a star and was gallivanting around the galaxy on its own terms. She had finally managed to locate it and that is where she had been dropped off, having overstayed her welcome on the freighter. The lines converged at this point; she was sure of that. If she was wrong, she had condemned herself to die in the darkness of this planet with no sun.

Fifteen days later, after having wandered around the planet, following the signals on her instruments, she was on the verge of giving up, having exhausted her food and with only the last few drops of water left in her bottle.

That was when Inku had found her lying against a rock. She must have dozed off for a bit, when she was woken up by a small cough to find him standing before her, gazing intently at her with those dark maroon eyes.

"Looks like you've found what you were seeking, Ms J'ron," he said smilingly.

"And…you are…?" Her voice was calm, but her heart pounded in her chest.

"Inku. No one has ever managed to reach this far, you know, that's why I kept my studio on this rogue planet, wandering about the galaxy with no ties binding me to any one place. Come, I think you'll be more comfortable in my workshop." He spoke J'ron's language with a perfect accent.

She got up, gathered her instruments as well as her backpack and followed him home.

His studio turned out to be the most advanced laboratory she had ever seen in her life. Hell, I can't even imagine what most of these instruments are meant to do, she thought, as Inku handed her food and water, exactly the same as she would have back home. She swallowed hungrily feeling strength return to her body. Even as she ate, she looked around the lab, a thousand questions erupting in her mind.

Inku sat across from her smiling indulgently. She finally felt embarrassed, finished eating, drank some water and sat back.

"It is remarkable that you are the first being who has managed to crack my elaborate scheme."

"I was right, wasn't I? All life in our galaxy originated artificially from a single point. In fact, from this very planet!"

"Yes, you were right, I created all intelligent life."

"What? Why? How? It takes millions of years as far as we know. Even though it was my theory, I cannot believe the truth though," she gestured at him, "it's standing right in front of me. Are you… God?"

"God? No." He laughed heartily. "I'm no God. I'm just part of an ancient civilization. Millions of years ago we spread across various galaxies tasked with spreading living energy. Come, I'll show you." Inku got up and walked across the vast hall.

She followed him meekly, overwhelmed. Millions of years old? Was he joking?

Inku stood in front of a large apparatus with a large glass window containing some sort of a fluid. "This is where I create my concoction of DNA, with suitable trigger events which will enable the entity to evolve into an intelligent, self-procreating life form. I then find suitable planets and launch the capsule, calculating and optimising for the eons of distance it must travel to the host planet. And then," his eyes twinkled, "I simply wait for the magic to happen!"

He moved to another console. "In case you were wondering, here is the genetic profile I used to create your species, approximately sixty million years ago. I am rather pleased with the result, seeing that you cracked my code."

She ran her hand over the console. Her species had not evolved on T'ref'ker, after all; it had come from elsewhere. But the thought that it had actually been created, here on this planet, left her dumbstruck. Whatever wild theories she had worked on, intelligent design had not been one of them. She somehow composed herself to ask the next logical question. "You say you create intelligent life, but not all life?"

"That is correct. Life is for God to create, and we have not yet determined His existence. But intelligent life modelled after our own, that I can do. Here, would you like to try one? I generally create a new species every million years of so, so many delicate calculations to be carried out, you know. However, this one is almost ready, and you can give it the finishing touches. I've even located the planet, a blue-green member around a yellow star, crowded with a life form I call reptilian. I intend to use those reptiles as the foundation for my next project." He looked sombre. "They are due for an extinction level event." Then he smiled again, like a kindly grandfather indulging his favourite grandchild. "Come along then, we have a narrow window of opportunity when all the stars are aligned just right."

She moved as if in a daze, following his instructions and inputting commands to modify the

DNA they were supposed to launch. She made a few changes to ensure the final form would look similar to her own.

"It is complete? We will now take it to the launch capsule. Here, hold it, will you?" He handed her the small capsule. "Yes, just like that. Go ahead, take it to the launcher and well… launch it," he gently prodded her.

"You really want me to do this?"

"Yes, I do. It is fitting actually, now that you have found me and my little secret, and there is no way you can go back home, even if I allowed you to. There is only one option left to you—to remain here as my apprentice. You do realise that you will give birth to a whole new species, don't you? You did design them somewhat like you, right? Bipedal, walking-erect, two genders. Five stages of evolution? Your people were right about evolution, partly anyway. I, and now you, create the templates and then the life form starts evolving from that point onwards." Seeing her hesitate, he pointed to the capsule in her hand. "Would you like to name them?" he asked simply.

She stared in wonder at the capsule, bright and glittering, velvety to touch. She held the seeds of life in her hand. "I will call them 'human' after the mountains on my own planet and yes, I will be their 'Mother'!"

She placed the capsule in the launcher and pressed the button to send it on its way home.

BOÖTES

The closed curtains, the dimmed lights, the soft murmur of the life-support machines— the room smelled of impending death. I felt pity for the old thaisa lying on the bed, wasting away. He had asked to meet me one last time. Alone. I did not know what to make of the request. My grandfather and I had been close once, sharing a love for physics, but then I had moved on to other worlds to carry on my research, while the old man had moved in with my parents, too weak to work, too old to stay alone. That will be me one day.

I entered the room and went to the bed. I stood by the bedside, looking upon the thin body lying beneath the sheets. A single tube snaked its way into the bulbous nose, supplying life-giving air. I sat on the edge of the bed and ran my hand over the few wiry hairs left on the skull of the person I lovingly called 'gramps'. He showed no reaction. I gently shook his shoulder.

He opened his eyes and turned his head, taking time to focus on my face. He smiled weakly when he saw me.

"You came?" His fingers shook as he reached for my hand.

"Yes, gramps. How are you doing?"

"Come closer, Serex," he said in a whisper, barely audible over the sound of the medical instruments. A weak pull on my hand reinforced his request.

I leaned in closer.

"I have decided that you are the only one in this family who can know the truth," he began. "Maybe you can find a way to stop it."

I was intrigued, to say the least. Gramps had been a scientist of some reputation back in his days and had completed many a trip across the galaxy researching stellar phenomena, but I had never taken him for a cloak-and-dagger person. I was suddenly eager to hear his story.

"Sixty-five years ago, I led an unsanctioned mission to the Boötes constellation. My fellow scientists and I were going to examine the supervoid in that region of space. You know what supervoids are, of course."

I nodded. Sure, I knew about supervoids. They were regions of space completely devoid of any galaxies or celestial bodies, with temperatures nearing the absolute zero. The closest one was at least three hundred million light years across. It was in Boötes, 700 million light years away. So, the old man had travelled that far.

"What you don't know is how the supervoid was formed, and more importantly…" he paused to take a ragged breath, "how it will affect us within a few years."

I waited for him to continue.

"No, I should start from the beginning," he said. "It all started when I was sent to Diuq to interview an alien as part of a top-secret government project. She was one of the last of her species. As I debriefed her, her revelations shocked me. She was from an empire in Boötes, which spanned millions of light years across many galaxies. They were at war with another galactic empire, both matched in size and strength.

Their war dragged on for thousands of years resulting in the destruction of countless planets and the slaughter of billions. Then around two hundred years ago, a Diuq scientist developed a compound that worked like a perfect black body." He stopped to catch his breath. It was clear that speaking so much was taxing his fragile system. I got up and fetched him some water. He managed to swallow a sip and sighed. "I don't have much time left. Our planet's future will depend on you. Promise me you will do whatever it takes to stop this monstrosity."

I had no idea what gramps was talking about, but I nodded dutifully. At least I understood the physics behind the old man's story. Black bodies absorbed every bit of radiation that fell on them, whether it was light, heat or any other type.

"Yes? Good. So, this scientist developed a perfect black body and the Diuq deployed it as a weapon. It was even better than a black hole, as the Diuq thought they would be able to control it. They deployed many such black bodies across their enemies' empire. Then, disaster struck. The black bodies took a life of their own. They pulled in all radiation, reducing temperatures across the sector to near zero. It was so cold that all motion seized, even at the level of quarks. Entire regions of space were rendered barren and lifeless, and the blackness continued to expand until it enveloped its creators. Everything was destroyed; entire civilizations wiped out. However, the devastation did not stop there. The black bodies merged to form this supervoid." A tear rolled down his cheek and he grew silent. I gently wiped it away and waited. "This void continues to grow, and our last study indicated that it was expanding at an accelerating rate. Soon, it will consume everything in this galaxy as well. Everything. That, Serex, will be the end of life."

I took a deep breath, stunned by what he had told me. "What would you want me to do, gramps? Did you work out how it can be stopped?"

He shook his head slightly. "The last time, sixty-five years ago, when our ship reached the edge of the void, we tested it. We got no readings. It did not register on our instruments at all. For all purposes, it did not exist. Our ship did manage to touch its growing boundary, and it sucked in all our energy. Our life support failed and everyone on that ship died, except me. I somehow managed to reach a research outpost. The government seized my ship and classified all my findings. I was sent off to an obscure posting and all knowledge of the event was removed.

Since then, all research into the phenomenon has been…shall we say, 'discouraged'?"

I nodded. I had always wondered about it—the incredible amount of red tape one needed to navigate through even for the most basic study of the void, the restrictions on travel to that region of space. It all made sense now. Could this be a galactic level conspiracy?

Gramps said, "I continued my research, though, and I have reason to believe that the void will consume our system within a few years. Its rate of acceleration will continue to grow exponentially. You, my grandson, must find a way to convince the government to remove the restrictions." His voice grew hoarse, yet insistent. "Stop it before it is too late."

***

The sky was the deepest black ever witnessed by anyone. It had been many years since we had seen even a single star at night. In fact, day and night had merged as the supervoid continued to mushroom. We were literally in the dark ages. The sun itself had disappeared a few days ago, consumed by the void and the world awaited its fate. The government had finally acknowledged the threat, but it was too little too late. There was no escaping the darkness. Every ship, every probe we had sent towards it had been instantly rendered inert. We had no contact with the other colonies or planets. No one knew what happened inside the void. Was it full of dead planets and dead bodies floating around in absolute darkness? How cold is absolute zero? Can one spend an eternity frozen in space?

This was one death of the Universe that no one had predicted. I did not look forward to this one death. It was meaningless. It left nothing behind. No essence of life. No essence of science. No essence of art. No one to lament your loss. Nothing.

I looked up at the sky again as the darkness grew deeper and deeper and deeper.

Sorry, gramps. I failed you.

BLACK
DEATH

Phil fingered the golden badge on his chest. It said 'TTA' in black letters inset in a golden arrow that curved to form a circle. The arrow represented the philosophy of the Time Travel Authority that time was a closed loop curve and cause and effect were forever linked together. If we changed the past, we would change the future. Phil worked at TTA as a temporal history agent. He enjoyed his job, going back in time to study historical events. Of course, travelling forward into the future was not possible. That barrier was yet to be broken.

Entering his workplace, Phil waved hesitantly at Brenda. She had joined the team a year back, but he had never managed to progress beyond casual greetings. Maybe someday he would muster the courage to ask her out.

His schedule had been posted to his communicator that morning—year 1347, location Moscow, Medieval Europe. This was exciting. He'd never been to that part of Earth before or even that era. The ancient middle ages were definitely not for the faint-hearted. He stepped into the briefing room and was surprised to find Dr Klaus waiting for him, instead of his boss, the formidable Ms Xan. Klaus had joined the agency only a few weeks back and Phil knew very little about his background. There was something furtive about his behaviour and Phil did not trust him. But the man had the right credentials and had had a meteoric rise in the field of temporal mechanics. His knowledge about the intricacies of time travel was uncanny.

"All ready, Phil?" asked Klaus. Phil nodded.

"Good, here're your briefing papers. You'll spend just under twenty-four hours following the land trade routes from Moscow to Prague, Munich and Paris, all the way to London. Spend a few hours at each location gathering your data and then come back. Study the details well. All the best."

Phil's shoulders sagged. Follow trade routes? Seriously? Here he had been hoping for a real adventure. This sucked royally. He looked around to see if he could locate Ms Xan but it seemed she was not on the floor that morning. He briefly considered giving her a call to check the assignment, but the rotating lights came on just then, indicating the travel capsule was ready to go. Might as well get it over it, he thought with a sigh. Who knew, if he was lucky maybe something exciting would turn up. He donned his isolation suit and entered the travel chamber. Seating himself in the only chair in the room, he turned and gave a thumbs up to the technician, who pressed a button. The room dissolved slowly around Phil.

***

Late from her meeting, Ms Xan walked rapidly to the travel chamber.

"Who was that who left just now?"

The technician got up so suddenly, he nearly pressed the abort button.

"Mr Phil, ma'am. Travel schedule number 2 as posted this morning?"

Dr Klaus tapped Ms Xan on the shoulder. "We discussed this, Ms Xan. He's making a quick trip to gather some data for the research group over at the Vinci Museum."

Xan looked annoyed. "Where and when? Why wasn't I consulted?"

"I... I didn't think it necessary for a low-risk jump."

She glared at Klaus. He had been taking too many liberties based on his celebrity status. "Time and location?" She asked sternly.

"1347, Moscow," the technician answered, wondering if he had made a mistake.

"What? But that was the time of the bubonic plague! Why would you send him there?"

"Relax, Ms Xan," said Klaus. She visibly flinched at the casual way he took her name. "I know what I am doing. He will be fine in his isolation suit."

***

Phil hated the filthy condition of medieval cities and Moscow was no different. His suit filtered out the bacteria, viruses and harmful volatiles but he could almost feel the dreadful stink all around him. He checked his suit again out of force of habit, grateful that it rendered a sterile environment within, while keeping him invisible.

He looked around. Something was wrong. It was almost mid-day and yet the streets were empty. A couple of stray dogs roamed about but nothing else moved. *Shit! I should have read the briefing docs more carefully.* He went from street to street, searching for signs of life. He turned a corner and stopped short. Countless bodies in various stages of decay were heaped in the centre of the large open square.

Something touched his foot and he jumped. *Just a bloody rat.* He kicked out with his foot sending the rat scuttling away. He felt another movement on the right. Another rat and another and another; the place was suddenly teeming with the vermin. *Oh my God! This is the time of the bubonic plague. The Black Death. What the hell has Klaus sent me into? More rats! Where are these creatures coming from?* He looked around wildly as rats surrounded him on all sides, a couple of bold ones actually gnawing at his suit. He ran, slipping and falling repeatedly, feeling the squelching of small bodies crushed under his feet. *Damn this mission!* Unable to take it anymore, he pressed a button and the horrifying scene disappeared.

***

He reappeared in Prague, as his location beacon proclaimed. A city as dirty as the previous one but thankfully full of people. His checked his suit quickly. It was intact as far as he could determine. He hoped the rats had not bitten and made tiny holes in the airtight suit. Also, he was still effectively invisible. *This is manageable. What the—* there was a crack on his controller console. *I must have damaged it while running away from the filthy creatures. God! Please let it work again.*

He glanced at his legs. His shoes were covered in blood. If anyone saw the blobs of blood floating abound mid-air, it would be a disaster. He stepped to the side of the road and scraped his shoes on the edge of a filth-strewn gutter trying to get as much of the blood and specks of fur off. Then he put his foot in the gutter to allow the dirty water to wash off the remaining blood.

That's it. I am out. He pressed the button again. Nothing happened. He looked around in desperation. If his console had conked off, he would never escape this godforsaken place. He pressed it again and again and again. The console beeped and he disappeared.

Rats are drawn to the smell of blood, even if it belongs to their own kind. This rat was a fine specimen of his kind. It swam in the dirty water, found the blobs of blood and licked them off. A few flecks of fur stuck to its snout. The rat moved on, blissfully ignorant of the ticks attached to the fur from the previous rat.

***

Phil reappeared at a new time and place. *The scene seems familiar, but how? Looks like some place I have seen in ancient black-and-white videos.* His console was acting up again. He tapped the display. It flickered on. *This can't be right! June 1947, Sarajevo, Bosnia and Herzegovina? What the hell? Had his vigorous tapping activated multiple jumps in time and space? At least I am still on Earth. How much time has really passed since I came back in time? Hours? Days? He did not know. All he knew was that he was hungry and tired.*

He walked down the street, trying to avoid the crowds. He needed to find a watch shop somewhere. That was the likeliest place he could think of that might have some tools to repair his console. A hubbub behind him made him turn. *Looks like some kind of a parade.* He could have checked the details on his console, but it was acting weird again.

He tried to keep as still as possible as the people swarmed past him. He briefly considered entering a nearby deli and keep a low profile, but his thoughts were interrupted as a murmur rose in the crowd. A group of cars had suddenly turned a corner and entered the street. They were moving at what he thought would be considered high speed for that time period. He noticed the occupants of the vehicles were dressed in military uniforms or royal regalia. *Sophie and Archduke Ferdinand! How much worse is it going to get? I am caught in the cusp of a significant historical moment. I must not interfere or cause any change. It will alter history for all time to come.* His desperation grew.

The cars came closer, the people in the street waving to the royals. Someone in one of the cars called out suddenly and the cars stopped right in front of Phil. *This is the moment. I have to get out of here.* Phil turned to run and collided into the man behind him who was drawing a pistol from his coat. The man dropped his gun, cursed and bent to pick it up. Someone in the crowd screamed. A military person jumped off from the first car, came running and tackled the armed man, throwing him to the ground. The cars immediately started up and sped away. A crowd gathered, beating the man black and blue.

Phil ran. He had just interrupted a major moment in history. Ms Xan would have his head for that, if she still existed, and if he could get back to his time.

He banged the console hard and was surprised to see it work. He punched the code to return and disappeared, leaving behind the jeering crowd and a bloodied man being carried off by the police.

***

I am back! Phil wanted to shout triumphantly. He stood up, waiting for the decontamination to be completed. A fine mist of disinfectants and fumigants sprayed on his suit and filled the room. The floor became wet and the wastewater flowed down the drain. High velocity air-dried off the suit. When the airflow stopped, he pulled off his suit and dropped it in the disposal bin, which carried it off to be incinerated. Pushing open the door of the travel pod, he stepped out.

Everything looked normal. The technician at the controls waved at him. Phil gave him a thumbs up. Klaus and Xan were standing together in the room.

"You see? He is all right," said Klaus to Xan and motioned for Phil to join him in the briefing room.

Xan dismissed the incident and moved off. She decided she would confront the SOB if he crossed the line again. Klaus closed the door of the briefing room behind Phil.

"I have a confession to make, Doc," said Phil, eager to get it off his chest.

"I know what you did in Moscow and Prague." Klaus smiled. "In fact, I sent you back for the same purpose, to spread the plague."

"You… you sent me back to spread the plague. Why? Why would you do that?"

Klaus shrugged. "There is no harm in telling you this. You just proved my theory: time is a closed loop curve, but the events in human history do not affect the flow of time and the outcome will always adjust itself even if the events themselves are interfered with by going into the past."

"What do you mean? Of course they do. That is why we have the isolation suits, so that we don't contaminate the timeline or bring anything back which can contaminate ours. You are delusional. I have to talk to Ms Xan."

"Hold on. Hold on. Hear me out, okay?"

Phil crossed his arms and looked at him suspiciously.

Klaus straightened a few objects on the desk thoughtfully, as if he were questioning his own decision to share the secret with Phil. Then apparently having made up his mind, he faced Phil. "I'm from your future and with your trip I have definitively proven that whatever humans do, they cannot influence time. I had sent a researcher back and he stopped the spread of the plague but then it was deemed as interference and my future experiments were forestalled. I wanted to send him back and rectify the timeline and prove again that time is immortal; events will readjust to the present reality, whatever changes you make to the past. However, with my approvals taken away, I had to try something different."

Klaus looked self-satisfied, even smug. "This is where you come in. I decided to come back in time and try out my luck with you. And as you can see, it worked. My first experiment of stopping a crucial human historical event resulted in no major change in the long-term history over the next five hundred years, well into your future and my present. Time moved on. And using you I restored the timeline again with no significant change again." His eyes shone.

He is right. I spread the plague. My action will cause millions to die. His head spun with the implications. *But in the process, I also stopped an assassination. I stopped World War I, and probably World War II as well. And the atrocities of the Nazis? I saved millions of lives. But, does this mean someone will have to be sent back in time to cause millions of deaths?* He had no answers. If there was one thing he knew for certain, it was this: *Klaus used me. He used me!*

"Time is endless and we humans are too pitiful to affect time. This is huge! Don't you understand what this means?" Klaus continued, not noticing Phil's expression.

"Not really, no. I do not understand." Phil was livid at having been treated as a pawn in an experiment. Suddenly, he shivered. He was beginning to feel cold. A sense of dread filled him. There was a strange taste in his mouth. He put in a finger; it came out wet with blood.

"Oh. Will you look at that?" He pushed the finger in Klaus's face, who flinched. "Looks like the decontamination did not work. I wonder what else I carried back with me. Welcome to hell, Doctor Klaus!" He leaped forward and coughed directly into Klaus's face. "Let's see what this little experiment of mine reveals about *your* future!"

AFTERMATH

Year 2320

Fourth planet, Bernard star system, 5.9 light years from Earth

"They're launching another volley of rockets," Mia called out. "Impact in twenty seconds."

"That's the fifth time in the last hour. When will they learn?" remarked Jared from the next station. "Their thermonuclear missiles are bloody useless against our ships."

They studied their screens, not bothering to brace for the expected impact. The nuclear missiles from the surface of planet 56 Bg A exploded harmlessly against the shields of the massive Earth ships.

These strikes were more like using a fly swatter against a whale. The warheads exploded harmless, their energy dissipating off into space. They had to be getting frustrated, if not downright desperate, to keep trying a failed tactic. It was sad.

"I know what you are thinking, Mia," said Jared. "They are desperate. Just listen to the radio chatter coming from the surface. Their pitiful satellites are gone. They have no ships capable of reaching us in high orbit. They were unprepared for our assault, exactly as Intelligence had suggested."

"Pipe down, you two," came the stern voice of the strike force commander. "Focus on the task at hand. We have less than twenty-four hours before the mining ships arrive. The surface has to be prepared for their arrival. Signal the other ships. We strike in one hour. Pattern gamma. Synchronise the systems and be ready to link all ships and assume control at T minus fifteen minutes."

"This is Mike Leader to Mike 2, 3 and 4. Prepare to strike. Counting down T minus sixty minutes." Jared received the acknowledgements and reported to the commander. "Mike 2, 3 and 4 report ready, ma'am."

"Roger. Mia, prepare strike pattern gamma. Sixteen warheads each ship, maximum yield."

"Yes, ma'am." She dialled up the numbers. A strike of that magnitude would be enough to obliterate the roughly two billion humanoids of the post-industrial civilization on the surface, along with all of the animal life on land. Life in the oceans would survive for some years till the contaminated water finished it off. The surface clean up, post the strike, would not take more than a few weeks for the massive mining ships. The ocean resources could wait until the surface had been stripped of all useful minerals. Over time, the planet would not only be left lifeless but devoid of its crust and significant parts of the mantle.

"Jared," she called, keeping her voice low. "Why are we not using neutron bombs this time?"

"I heard the bosses discussing it. When they used neutron bombs in Alpha Centauri, the population was vaporised yet the cities were unharmed. It took many months to clear out the cities, remove all the debris and begin mining. That cost a lot of money. This time they decided to go all out and save the time."

"So, as if it weren't bad enough that we're killing the entire population, we are now going to destroy every trace of their entire civilisation?"

"Hey, don't blame me. Blame the bureaucrats who came up with the plan." Jared raised his hands in mock surrender. "Besides we have no other way if we want Earth to prosper. And I certainly don't mind the little bonus we will get if this is done on schedule." He turned away, apparently satisfied with his reasoning. "Besides, this is far easier than trying to colonise the natives. That takes too many resources and almost never turns out well."

She turned to her screen. This was not right. She may just be a rookie pilot, but this would be the fourth wave of destruction that Earth would be bringing upon the sentient civilisations near the solar system. There had been no efforts made to understand how life evolved on different planets or to extend a hand of friendship. In the beginning, fifty years ago, it had been seen as a matter of survival. Earth needed evermore resources and the entire solar system had already been stripped bare. Now, with progress made using other planets' minerals, Earth was prosperous once again. Now, it was just a matter of minting more money. It was pure greed.

She pulled up a transmission from the surface. It was audio-visual. Panicked crowds trying to escape crowded city centres—the entire surface was in chaos. She looked around the control room surreptitiously, then turned on the camera and focussed it on the city directly below them. It was one of the largest on the planet. She zoomed in. Individual people came into focus. Quite unlike what they had found on Alpha Centauri, she mused, and yet beautiful, vulnerable. And in another hour, they would all be dead. Not just dead, obliterated. Vaporised. Back at the training centre, they had said that it would be a fast and merciful death. Nevertheless, it was still death. There was a finality to it. Was it right to destroy whole civilisations for your own survival? Possibly. But was it right to destroy whole civilisations just so the fat cats back on Earth could get fatter, ride a bigger craft, take even fancier vacations on Europa?

She looked around the room. Everyone was busy or pretending to be. For many of them this would be the third or even fourth mission. They were veterans, possibly immune to death by now. One death shocks you, two are difficult to handle emotionally, ten deaths are a tragedy. Billions of deaths are just statistics. Empty numbers.

She continued to watch the scene being played out below on a small portion of her screen. She could almost grasp some of the emotions being displayed. The gentle touching of tentacles between groups of individuals. The lowering of the heads in defeat. The running around in panic.

They may be primitive but they are alive. Life in the universe may not be as sparse as we believed two hundred years back, but it is still rare. And habitable planets? You can count them on your fingertips. Yet, humans have learned nothing. Barely escaping the destruction of our own world through mismanagement, now we are bringing death to other worlds. But what can I do alone? Something stirred in her memory. A phrase often repeated in schools back on Earth. 'If you can't feed a hundred people, then feed just one.' *If I can't save a hundred planets, how about I save just one?*

The commander had asked to set pattern gamma. That would deploy missiles evenly to cover the entire land area of the planet below. *What if I can change it to target the other ships?* The very thought was treason, she knew. She felt weak in the knees. But she pulled herself together. *I can make it work. I just need to hide the firing pattern from curious eyes until the time is on hand.* Mia glanced at the countdown time. *Or maybe there is another way which will be even easier. Forty-two minutes to go. More than enough time.* She set to work.

The last wave of missiles from the surface broke through the dark clouds. They rose lethargically towards the four ships, as if they were giving up the quest as futile even before reaching their targets. Mia kept her eye on the small window in the corner of her screen showing the camera feed. The people on the planet surface were all looking towards the sky. She could almost sense the hope in their eyes as they followed the smoky path of the missiles, which had disappeared into the clouds.

"Six missiles aimed at us, and an equal number on each of the other ships" she called out. "Impact in fifteen seconds."

"This is the last volley, people. We will ride this out and then call our own strike. Once this is over, drinks at the bar are on me," called out the commander, relaxing in her chair.

Mia felt a twinge of doubt as she considered what she was about to do. It would be suicide and murder. Murder of her own people, including some of her closest friends. She wondered if anyone would ever find out what she had done. *Well, hopefully my last message will reach Earth someday and better sense will prevail.*

Mia pressed the button to bring down the shields on all the ships just at the missiles exploded.

An absurd thought came to her mind at the very last moment. A final wish for the people she had just saved on the planet below. Something she remembered from ancient broadcasts.

Live long and...

BLACK HOLES HAVE HAIR

The console chimed indicating an incoming message. Uge turned from his experiment and looked at the screen.

Hello, Uge. The letters glowed green on the screen against the red and gold light flowing in through the portholes.

Hello, Uge? He scratched his chin in confusion. The next transmission from the home base was not due for another 56 hours. So, who was this?

He walked back to the main console. *Source of transmission unknown,* reported his computer.

'*Hello, Uge*' continued to glow on the screen. He sat down, looking at the message with furrowed brows.

A soft beam of blue light shone briefly outside drawing his attention. It seemed to have come from the black hole he had been observing. Two hundred and twenty days alone in space have scrambled my brain, Uge decided.

The letters on the screen changed: *Uge, I am out here, and I need your help.*

Okay, I am officially going crazy, Uge thought, staring at the message. There was nothing outside except the black hole, with the swirling matter and energy, which formed its accretion disc. He turned off the screen.

Uge, please respond. The screen switched on again.

Uge waited a moment thinking if he should respond. Oh, what the hell! He started typing. *Hello, there. Who is this?*

I am the entity you refer to as M92.*

That is the designation of this black hole, more properly known as Gravitationally Completely Collapsed Object or GCCO for short, responded Uge. *And black holes can't communicate. So, I ask you again. Please identify yourself.*

I am M92. I am the black hole.*

This is nuts, thought Uge. Someone seems to have played a time-delayed prank on my computer system. He pushed a few buttons and rebooted the computer.

From the corner of his eye, he saw another short burst of blue outside. The computer booted up and instead of the welcome screen, there were the words again: *Hello, Uge.*

You are still here? Who are you and what do you want?

I have told you already. I am M92 and I need some knowledge. Will you help me?*

Guess there is no harm seeing how this plays out, thought Uge. *Sure. What do you need?*

I need to understand your thesis on the merger of black holes. There are some references in your computer's database but the details are missing.

Why would you want to know about that?

That does not concern you.

If you want my help, then yes, it does concern me. Typed Uge.

The screen remained blank. Good riddance, thought Uge, getting up to fix himself a beverage.

I have considered it. Your request is reasonable. M92* or whoever it was had finally responded.

You think? *So tell me why and tell me how you can communicate with me. You are an inanimate object.*

Inanimate? M92* seemed to struggle to come up with a response. *That is not correct. I have knowledge. I have vast amounts of it. I gather everything that reaches me and store all that I need at my event horizon. It has been so for millions of years. Signals from distant planets, data from stellar phenomenon. I know everything.*

Then it is surprising that you do not know how black holes merge.

M92* was silent. *That is correct. Information comes to me in bits and pieces. The earliest bits coalesced together many years ago and gave me a rudimentary intelligence. Since then it has grown to a vast amount. Yet, some information simply does not reach me or is lost in the maelstrom you see outside.*

I see, replied Uge. Looks like I am invested. So, the theory was correct. Black holes do have other characteristics unique to them other than just mass, charge and angular momentum. Black holes can store additional information which may not be visible to anyone else, and this can be released and manifests as strands of ghostly particles much like the blue beams M92* used to exchange data with him. Black holes *do* have hair just as the scientists had predicted! Furthermore, if he was not dreaming, then this was his moment in the sun, proof that information does not get destroyed as it enters a black hole's event horizon. In fact, this new knowledge meant his people could actually work on creating an entirely new range of artificial intelligence. AIs may not even need programming. You could keep throwing information at an AI and it would make its own sense out of the information, growing as it absorbs more and more, just like M92* and ultimately the AI would also gain sentience.

Let me test if you are telling me the truth, he typed.

Yes. Ask me anything you want. And then you must give me the answer I seek.

Alright, here goes nothing. I'll ask M92* something no one else can know. *What is at your core, your centre? Is it a singularity?*

That is not entirely true. At my core, I have frozen time.

Frozen time? What the hell is that?

It is time that is frozen. What do you not understand?

Uge took a deep breath. *I mean, what exactly is frozen time?*

Words flashed rapidly across the screen and Uge struggled to read them.

Slow down a bit, will you? The flow reduced and he concentrated; his beverage growing cold by his side.

In the beginning, the universe was completely devoid of all matter, anti-matter and time did not flow. When the universe came into being at the moment you call the Big Bang, it released particles, which formed matter. It also released linear time. Not in a single burst but in pockets. Some of these pockets merged to form black holes. I contain pockets from the primal universe, protected by gravity. I have collected more and more of such pockets as they travelled through space. If you do find a way to enter me—and I can tell you how—you can re-live every single moment from the Big Bang to now. You can travel to every part of the universe without ever leaving me. I can tell you how, if you share your knowledge with me.

Uge tried to digest this. We always thought black holes contained gravity. But this guy says they contain time. Frozen time.

Hello, Uge.

He ignored the message.

Hello, Uge. What do you say?

I say yes. Here, let me send you the data. He typed the core equations. It was all based on quantum entanglement. *You, M92*, just need to find your quantum cousin formed at the exact same moment as you were, who shares your quantum properties. I have quite a* *few details about other black holes with me. Maybe we can find you the match.*

I understand now. It is so elegant and yet so simple.

Is it? Now, you keep your part of the deal.

Yes. You may enter. Look outside and you will see the path.

Uge looked out of the porthole. The donut around the black hole was splitting. The swirling rings seemed to collapse into themselves. All movement ceased. The sea had split and the path inside was clear. At the end of the path, at the very centre of the black hole, strange lights swirled in a mesmerizing display of pyrotechnics. Almost in a trance, Uge turned his ship and followed the path. He was absorbed into the black hole and so was his essence.

Yes. I understand everything now. Your bodies are minute, but your intellect is vast. But there is something else. What is this thing you call emotion? It is not clear. It is abstract and it changes. Intriguing. You ask me why I want to merge. I was wondering the same. Now I understand. It is emotion. I am lonely. I need a mate. We need to multiply. To spread our species. What is this you say? That I am not alive? That I cannot procreate? You are wrong. A few minutes ago, it was true. I could not procreate. I did not even know what it meant. Yet, with your emotion, I feel the need. The urge to multiply. I also feel something else. Power! I am the most powerful entity in the universe, and everyone must bow before me!

Dozens of relativistic jets shot out from M92*. Jets of immense power. Jets ready to destroy anything that came in their path.

THE
VEILED
UNIVERSE

"Bloody hell!" Adrian yelled, bringing an angry fist down on the panel. "That's five days of work down the drain, you stupid machine!"

Still cursing under his breath, he turned to reset the Notion Drive. The drive was the most powerful ever developed anywhere in the Universe, capable of propelling a ship at the speed of thought. Theoretically, he could travel billions of light years in an instant just by imagining his destination and synchronising it with the Drive. In practice, it was incredibly frustrating as the Drive and his thoughts constantly differed on their definition of the destination.

"Why do you keep bringing me back to where I started? I want to reach the edge of the universe, you bugger." Adrian banged his adjuster against the shiny cover of the drive. "Fifteen years of development down the drain, you…"

He gave up trying to fix the Drive and plonked himself down on the command chair, wiping the sweat from his brow. Adrian had no interest in the wonders that space had to offer in the distant reaches never seen by man. He just wanted to cross the boundary to behold what lay beyond the known Universe.

"Okay. Okay." He tried to calm down. All this swearing would give him a brain aneurysm soon. "Let's try this another way, alright," he said soothingly to the machine. More than brain waves linked them now. They were symbiotic. Inseparable. The Notion Drive was like a petulant child. He needed to be patient. "This is a simple matter of astrometry. If we keep coming back to the starting point every time we travel, then maybe the universe is closed, not open or flat. Maybe we need to start from the centre. Yes, that's it." He sat up straight and focussed, aligning his thoughts with the Notion Drive.

Centre of the Universe. Centre of the Universe.

There was a brief sensation of motion that stopped as abruptly as it had begun. He opened his eyes.

A blue-green planet gleamed in the darkness in front of him. His planet. *So, the ancient astronomers had been right, after all. Earth is the centre of the Universe. This really takes the cake.*

"Right then. Now we head outwards in a straight line. A perfect straight line, accounting for gravity and celestial bodies. And of course, black holes, dark matter, dark energy and what not. Let's leg it!"

This time the ride was just a little bit longer, with a few more bumps than usual. Adrian did not open his eyes for some time. He just sat there breathing deeply. If this had not worked—

The ship stopped and Adrian saw a barrier outside but it was translucent and shimmering like a soap bubble. The shimmering film stretched as far as he could see. It was like a sheer wall and his ship nudged it slightly, sending a shiver down his spine. The film moved away and his ship followed. The universe was expanding! Right in front of his eyes.

"Brilliant. Now, we will cross this barrier into another universe. That's all I had been asking you to do this whole time!" He closed his eyes. The ship moved forward slowly. He could almost feel it trying to break through something similar to a stretching membrane—soft but unyielding. A little more pressure and the ship broke through.

He checked his control panel. It was resetting itself. He had done it! He had crossed the barrier into an entirely new place.

"And now, milady, take me to the centre of *this* universe," he commanded.

The blue-green planet shone in front of him. "This cannot be right. I said the centre of *this* universe, idiot. Not my own." The ship did not move. The planet slowly rotated in front of him on the screen.

I give up. Let's just go on home and have a nice sandwich for lunch.

The ship rocked violently. Adrian grasped the armrests. Another ship had appeared right next to his. It looked suspiciously familiar. His console chimed with an incoming message and an image appeared on the screen.

That's me!

"Hello, there, Adrian."

"Hello, yourself… Adrian." He was too numb to react.

"Looks like you've broken the thought barrier *and* the barrier of your universe! Congratulations. You are the fourth human to have done so. But, since all of them were you," he paused, "or me, I really don't know the difference."

Adrian found his voice. "You… you mean, there are more like me and you?"

"Yes, it would appear so. Like I said, I've met three others. As far as I can determine, this region where we are seems to be some sort of a focal point. All roads lead to Rome, as they say, and all our versions in all the universes seem to be congregating here."

"That's a load of bull. I'm off. Goodbye." Adrian closed his eyes and the ship jumped again. He opened them once they crossed a similar barrier. He was back near Earth only this time there were dozens of ships around him, all the same as his.

"Hello, Adrian." The call came in again, from dozens of voices in perfect synchronisation.

"Am I going mad?" he asked.

"Not really," the other Adrians answered in unison. "It seems multiverses do exist. Only that..." There was a long pause. He grew anxious to hear the answer. *Only what?*

"—every part of the multiverse is exactly the same. We broke the barrier between universes and this is what we have found. There are no alternate realities. There is no splitting of the universe every time you make a choice. All is one. We exist together, in parallel time frames, living out our lives in the exact same manner. There is only one path. That, Adrian, is the reality."

"No. I refuse to believe it. I have spent decades decoding the secrets of the Universe!" He was shouting without meaning to. "There has to be more. So much more. A multitude of dimensions. Boundaries we cannot reach. Even more exotic universes to discover beyond our own! How can there be only one reality? No. It is not possible. No. You are lying. Stop it."

He closed his eyes. The ship moved. He opened his eyes. He was near Earth. Another Earth. The same Earth. This time there were hundreds of ships crowing space. He closed his eyes.

Every repetition of the journey was the same. *I cannot accept this. I will not accept it.* He closed his eyes. He cried. He thought of home. *His* Earth. The ship moved.

***

"What's wrong with this one?" asked a voice on the other side of the glass window. He could hear them. The words sounded familiar but the meaning was lost.

The head physician consulted her notes. "Dr Adrian Cole, Department of Astrophysics, at the University. He has delusional disorder. He believes he invented a machine which could travel at the speed of thought and that he managed to travel across multiple universes. That is all we have been able to get out of him before he degenerates into nonsense."

"Is that so? What's the prognosis?"

"The damage seems to be deep. It is unlikely he will recover enough to tell us the whole story. However, there is one remarkable aspect—he was recovered from deep space from an escape capsule. They also found debris consistent with a small spaceship of some kind. So," she shrugged, "who knows, maybe he did find a way to travel far." She turned to face the visitor. "It is perhaps a warning to all of us. The universe is veiled and we may never really know all its secrets. Perhaps humans were never meant to understand it fully and even if they do find the truth, it turns them insane like Adrian here. Perhaps it is better this way."

Dear Reader

What a ride! Right?

If you enjoyed this book, do not forget to leave a review on Amazon and Goodreads.

Thank you and watch out for more!

Rob Garnet

www.ingramcontent.com/pod-product-compliance
Lightning Source LLC
La Vergne TN
LVHW042157190726
843493LV00006B/1715